Masters of Spinjitzu

LEGO® GRAPHIC NOVELS AVAILABLE FROM PAPERCUTZ

NINJAGO #1

NINJAGO #2

NINJAGO #3

NINJAGO #4

BIONICLE #1

BIONICLE #2

BIONICLE #3

BIONICLE #4

BIONICLE #5

BIONICLE #6

BIONICLE #7

BIONICLE #8

BIONICLE #9

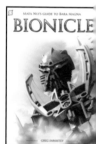

Mata Nui's Guide
to Bara Magna

#4 TOMB OF THE FANGPYRE

Greg Farshtey – Writer
Jolyon Yates – Artist
Jayjay Jackson – Colorist

New York

NINJAGO Masters of Spinjitzu
#4 "Tomb of the Fangpyre"

GREG FARSHTEY – Writer
JOLYON YATES – Artist
JAYJAY JACKSON – Colorist
BRYAN SENKA – Letterer

Production by NELSON DESIGN GROUP, LLC
Special thanks to ROBERTO GUEDES and STEVE DITKO
Associate Editor – MICHAEL PETRANEK
JIM SALICRUP
Editor-in-Chief

ISBN: 978-1-59707-329-5 paperback edition
ISBN: 978-1-59707-330-1 hardcover edition

Printed in China
December 2012 by Asia One Printing LTD.
13/F Asia One Tower
8 Fung Yip St., Chaiwan, Hong Kong

Distributed by Macmillan

Third Printing

MEET THE MASTERS OF SPINJITZU...

JAY

COLE

ZANE

KAI

And the Master of the Masters of Spinjitzu...

SENSEI WU

BEWARE!
YOU ARE ABOUT TO ENTER THE WORLD OF NINJAGO . . .

HA! **DANGER** IS MY MIDDLE NAME!

I THOUGHT YOU SAID YOU DIDN'T HAVE A MIDDLE NAME.

I BELIEVE HE HAS ONE, BUT IT'S SILLY.

ZIP IT, THE LOT OF YOU.

SENSEI, WHERE SHALL WE LOOK FOR THESE FRAGMENTS?

THEY WERE SCATTERED TO THE FOUR CORNERS OF NINJAGO. THESE WILL BE LONG AND DIFFICULT JOURNEYS, TO LANDS BEYOND IMAGINATION.

SOUNDS LIKE JUST ANOTHER DAY AT THE OFFICE.

INDEE

THE FIRST FRAGMENT CAN BE FOUND IN A LAND OF FIRE AND ICE, FAR TO THE SOUTH...

I'LL TAKE THAT ONE! JUST LET ME GET MY RIDE!

THIS WAY TO SERPENTINE STONE

OH, YOU'VE GOT TO BE KIDDING...

THIS WAY TO SERPENTINE STONE

IF SOMEONE WANTS ME GOING ONE WAY, I'M GOING THE **OTHER** WAY.

Later...

NO POINT SEARCHING IN THE DARK. I'LL MAKE A FIRE AND CAMP FOR THE NIGHT.

THERE WE GO, A NICE, BLAZING--

...*PIECE OF ICE.* HUH?

YIII!

A FROZEN FIRE AND RED-HOT SNOW? WHAT KIND OF A **CRAZY** PLACE IS THIS?

I *MUST* FIND A WAY TO DEFEAT THIS CREATURE, OR I WILL NEVER FIND MY STONE.

PERHAPS I CAN TRAP THE BEAST BETWEEN THOSE PILLARS LON ENOUGH TO GET WHAT I CAME FOR, AND ESCAPE!

CRUNNNCHM

AT LAST! I FEARED I WOULD NEVER ESCAPE FROM THAT-- OH, *NO!*

The power of the Golden Weapon of Spinjitzu causes a massive block of ice to form in the monster's jaws...

ITS POWERFUL JAWS WILL SHATTER THAT ICE IN AN INSTANT, BUT BY THAT TIME...

I WILL BE ON THE SURFACE...

...AND BACK ON DRY LAND. HERE'S HOPING MY FRIEND IS NOT AMPHIBIOUS.

NOW, WHAT TRUTHS DO YOU HAVE TO REVEAL, STONE?

"And the great serpent reached out with its power, and brought forth four tribes of snake-men on the world of Ninjago..."

"The fiendish Fangpyre ..."

"The criminal Constrictai ..."

"The hateful Hypnobrai..."

"And the vengeful Venomari."

"These four tribes of the Serpentine threatened to conquer Ninjago, and it seemed impossible to stop them."

"It took the creation of golden flutes to give the human inhabitants of this world the chance for victory."

"Using the flutes, the Serpentine were driven into tombs and sealed away... it was hoped, forever."

"But the Great Serpent was not defeated, merely delayed... and now it slumbers, waiting for the time when it will return again to menace Ninjago anew."

"And confident that none in this world know its secret."

IT WILL BE FASTER TO MAKE IT THROUGH ALL THIS RUBBLE IN THE TREAD ASSAULT.

WHOEVER THAT WAS I SAW, HE'S *FAST*. HE'S ALREADY OUT OF SIGHT.

"No, wait," says Cole. "There he is! He's trying to--"

KA-BAMM

CORRECTION, NOT 'TRYING TO,' HE *DID* DROP A BIG ROCK ON ME!

IT'S TIME HE AND I MET *FACE-TO FACE!*

In a daring move, Cole slams the tread assault into the wall...

CRASH

-:OOOF!:-

LLOYD GARMADON?! WHAT ARE YOU DOING HERE?

I'M HERE TO HELP YOU.

BY DROPPING A ROCK ON ME?

COME ON, LLOYD, WHY ARE YOU REALLY HERE?

THE FANGPYRE DON'T WANT YOU TO GET IT. ANYTHING THEY DON'T WANT, I DO WANT.

EXCELLENT! TWO DOWN, AND ONE TO GO-- FOOLISH FANGPYRE!

OH, NO!

AAAAAHHHH!

THE SNAKE WILL BE COMING BACK FOR ANOTHER PASS. SO MAYBE...

GET. ME. DOWN!

OWWWW!

WE'RE GOING FOR THE STONE, RIGHT NOW. WHERE IS IT?

I DON'T KNOW!

MAYBE THE SNAKES IN THOSE RATTLECOPTERS KNOW-- WANT TO GO BACK AND ASK?

OKAY, OKAY... MAYBE THEY SAID SOMETHING ABOUT UNDER THE ARCH.

LET'S GO, THEN, BEFORE THE FANGPYRE TRY SOMETHING ELSE.

None of them notice Cole unleashing his Spinjitzu power...

Not until it's *too late!*

GOT IT!

AND WE HAVE YOU!

TAKE THEM TO *THE TOMB!*

The Ninja's lucky streak seems to have come to an end, as Cole and Lloyd are marched off to the legendary tomb of the Fangpyre!

54

"When it wasss first touched by darknesss, the sssnake that would become the great ssserpent found its way into a garden."

"That brother wasss named Garmadon... and hisss terrible deedss would become legendary too."

"The Garden wasss home to two brothers. The sssnake took one by sssurprise and bit him, and by doing that, it passssed its darknesss onto him."

DO YOU SSSEE THE ANSWER NOW, HUMANSSS? DO YOU UNDERSSSSTAND THE POWER OF THE SSSECRET?

I DON'T GET IT. WHAT DOES ALL THIS HAVE TO DO WITH MY DAD?

I THINK I STARTING FIGURE IT CORRECT IF I'M WRO FANGTOM

"Garmardon fought his brother, Sensei Wu, and lost, being banished to the Underworld," explains Cole...

"Later, he unleashed skeleton armies on Ninjago and tricked my team into helping him escape his exile. He hasn't been seen since."

GARMADON LOST EVERYTHING WHEN HE TURNED BAD-- HIS BROTHER, HIS FREEDOM, AND EVEN NOW, HE HAS NOTHING BUT A DESIRE FOR POWER AND REVENGE.

BUT IF NONE OF THIS WAS REALLY HIS FAULT...

WHAT THE GREAT SSSERPENT CAN DO, IT CAN UNDO.

IN RETURN FOR AN ALLIANCE AND HISSS AID IN OUR CONQUESSST OF THIS MUDBALL PLANET, THE SSSERPENTINE CAN GIVE HIM BACK HISSS HONOR, HISSS FAMILY, ALL THAT HE DOESSS NOT HAVE NOW.

SO DAD WOULD HAVE TO DO SOMETHING REALLY BAD TO BECOME GOOD AGAIN?

AND ONCE HE WAS GOOD, HE WOULD FEEL TERRIBLE ABOUT WHAT HE HAD DONE FOR THE REST OF HIS LIFE.

IT'S A LOUSY DEAL, AND SINCE HE'S NOT HERE, I'LL ANSWER FOR HIM--

LLOYD
GARMADON

WATCH OUT FOR PAPERCUTZ ™

Welcome to the fourth, frightful LEGO® NINJAGO graphic novel from Papercutz, the company dedicated to publishing great graphic novels for all ages. I'm Jim Salicrup, Papercutz Editor-in-Chief and long-time Alice Cooper fan (despite his fondness for snakes). I'm here to tell you all about what's happening behind-the-scenes at Papercutz, and this time I have two really exciting announcements...

First, everyone at Papercutz wants to sincerely thank YOU for helping to make LEGO® NINJAGO the best-selling, all-ages graphic novel series for the early part of 2012, and at the rate we're going, possibly for all of 2012! Your support has helped land LEGO® NINJAGO #2 "Mask of the Sensei" in the #1 spot on the New York Times Best Selling Graphic Books (paperback) list the week it was released. Since then, both LEGO® NINJAGO #1 and #2 have remained in the top ten on that list, and as we go to press, based on advance orders, we suspect both LEGO® NINJAGO #3 and #4 will soon be included as well! Again, thank you so much. We greatly appreciate your support.

The other big story is that we have an amazing new artist onboard to draw the LEGO® NINJAGO graphic novel series, and his name is JOLYON YATES. Here's just a tiny bit of biographical information on this incredible artist:

Born in England, Jolyon Yates studied graphic design and illustration at Canterbury and Exeter, and Japanese arts in Sapporo, Japan, as a guinea pig in a college exchange program.

He lived in Japan for several years, during which time he contributed comics, articles and illustrations to magazines such as *Anime FX*. Jolyon also met his future wife there. He became a US citizen in 2008.

His first paid comics work was the story "Tancho" for *Mangazine*. He completed artwork for the award-winning web comic *Revvvelations* in 2010. Illustration work has included storyboards for commercials and movies and artwork for magazines and animation. He's been a regular contributor to *G-Fan*. He makes a brief appearance in the movie TENGU (2012), for which he drew character designs. He is very happy to be working on LEGO® NINJAGO but fears losing the ability to draw fingers, ears, and noses.

So, summing up, LEGO® NINJAGO is a hit, and Jolyon Yates will now be bringing Greg Farshtey's amazing scripts to life! And as exciting and action-packed as this graphic novel may be, wait till you see LEGO® NINJAGO #5 "Kingdom of the Snakes," coming soon to your favorite booksellers! Till then, don't miss out on any LEGO® NINJAGO news, by logging on to www.LEGO.com as often as possible, and stay on top of all the latest news from Papercutz at www.papercutz.com.

So, until next time, keep spinnin'!

Thanks,

Jim